WEiRDO2

EVEN WEIRDER!

Scholastic Press
345 Pacific Highway Lindfield NSW 2070
An imprint of Scholastic Australia Pty Limited (ABN 11 000 614 577)
PO Box 579 Gosford NSW 2250
www.scholastic.com.au

Part of the Scholastic Group
Sydney • Auckland • New York • Toronto • London • Mexico City
• New Delhi • Hong Kong • Buenos Aires • Puerto Rico

First published by Scholastic Australia in 2014.
Text copyright © Anh Do, 2014.
Illustrations copyright © Jules Faber, 2014.

National Library of Australia Cataloguing-in-Publication entry
Author: Do, Anh, author.
Title: WeirDo 2, even weirder / written by Anh Do ; illustrated by Jules Faber.
ISBN: 9781743622711 (paperback)
Target Audience: For primary school age.
Other Authors/Contributors: Faber, Jules, 1971-, illustrator.
Dewey Number: A823.4

Typeset in Grenadine MVB, Push Ups and Lunch Box.

Printed by RR Donnelley.
Scholastic Australia's policy, in association with
RR Donnelley, is to use papers that are renewable and
made efficiently from wood grown in sustainable forests,
so as to minimise its environmental footprint.

10 9 8 7 6 5 4 3 2 1   14 15 16 17 18 / 1

BLAH,
BLAH,
BLAH

ANH DO

Illustrated by JULES FABER

WEiRDO2
EVEN WEIRDER!

A SCHOLASTIC PRESS BOOK
FROM SCHOLASTIC AUSTRALIA

I was out shopping for a **birthday present** for the seventh-best-looking girl in the class. So why do I have five years' worth of **toilet paper** in the trolley?

Because

my life is
weird.

If something's on sale at the shops, Mum will buy <u>lots</u> of it.

And guess what was on sale today?

That's right,

toilet paper

There we all were . . . looking like

the family that does the

MOST POOS

in the world.

3

The fact is, we don't just use toilet paper in the toilet. We use it for other **stuff** around the house . . .

Like **blowing** your nose.

Wiping up **spills**.

escapee!

Ten Pin Rolling.

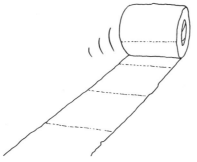

Did I tell you my mum was cheap? She's one of those people who gets a little too excited about the lady in the corner of the shop giving out the free sausage samples.

SMILE!

Mum will make us **all line up** for a taste, no matter what the sample is.

BROCCOLI BALLS?

YUMMO!

DUCK DONUT?

WOW WEE!

You're only allowed **one** sausage per person, but Mum makes us walk away and then come back looking slightly different, just to get **more food**.

And if the sausages are **REALLY** tasty, she'll make us come back one **extra time**.

GREAT!
NOW WE DON'T
HAVE TO WORRY
ABOUT LUNCH!

Roger's **the worst** at shopping. Somehow **strange stuff** always ends up in the trolley when he's around.

WHO BOUGHT THESE CHIPS
AND **JUMBO**
SAFETY PINS?

CHIPS
MEGA SIZE

SAFETY PINS

9

WHO BOUGHT THIS
ITCHY BUM
CREAM?

Anyway, there we were at the checkout with our

2000

rolls of toilet paper when I looked across
and saw... BELLA ALLEN!

HI WEIR!

HI BELLA.

'What are you buying?' she asked.

'We're just buying a … birthday present for you,'
I replied.

'Is that my present behind your back?' she asked with a smile.

'Oh no, that isn't for you either.'

I brought out the itchy bum cream to show her.

SEE? THIS IS JUST, UMM, JUST IN CASE . . . CHEAP TOILET PAPER CAN BE A BIT ROUGH SOMETIMES!

ITCHY BUM CREAM

What was I saying?!

'Okaaaaay, bye Weir,' she said.

NOOOOO!

Now Bella Allen thinks I am **the king** of **poo**. That I need a trolley full of toilet paper all for myself!

Can my life get any **worse**?

PRICE-CHECK ON **EXTRA-LARGE** ITCHY BUM CREAM FOR THE WEIRDO AT CHECKOUT 5.

My life just got worse!

Now the whole supermarket's looking at me!

How did the lady at the checkout know my name? Must have been

a lucky guess!

CHAPTER 2

My first name is **Weir**. My last name is **Do**. (Yep, rhymes with go.)

Just in case you missed my first book, let me tell you a little bit about me and my family.

Dad

Mum (cheap)

Granddad

Me

Roger

Sally

toilet paper

You already know I'm a **bit weird**. Like when they handed out **talents**, I wound up with . . .

And when they handed out **family hobbies** ...

And you already know that my mum is cheap.
She **really** is.

For **Roger's birthday**, instead of paying
for **real** helium balloons that float up to the
ceiling ...

... she just blew up plain balloons and then stuck them to the ceiling with sticky tape.

She's also one of those mums that makes us wear hand-me-down clothes. I got stuck with Sally's old school shoes ... but at least I didn't get her jumper!

My sister Sally is **super** neat. She does

everything
perfectly.

She even peels an orange all in **one go**.

perfect

And she's really good at making things, like **balloon** animals.

orange peel

Sally **never** makes a mess eating her noodles.

But me, I always seem to get that one long noodle that goes on and on forever!

At least I'm not as **messy** as Roger. Sometimes he even ends up with noodles **coming out of his nose**.

Roger is my little brother and he likes to **destroy stuff**. This week he's been **throwing** things into the bath. To **'clean'** them.

Often important things ...

CLEAN!

Mum refused to waste the soggy bread ... and I have to say, the **soggy sandwich** was one of the **worst three sandwiches** I've ever had in my life.

soggy sandwich

2nd worst sandwich (carrot and tomato)

Number 1 worst sandwich ever (pig ears)

My dad is just plain strange.

He can do a burp that lasts for a looooo

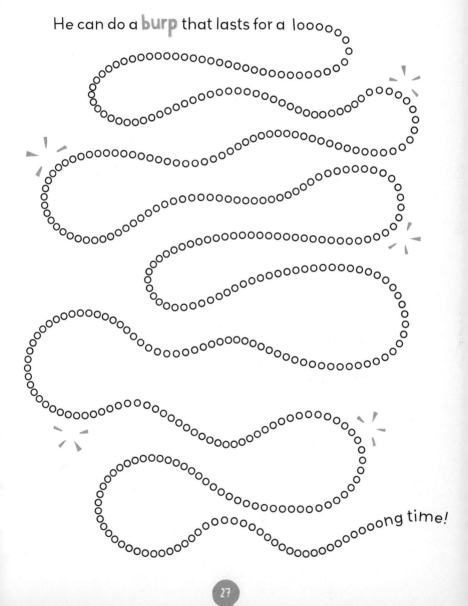

oong time!

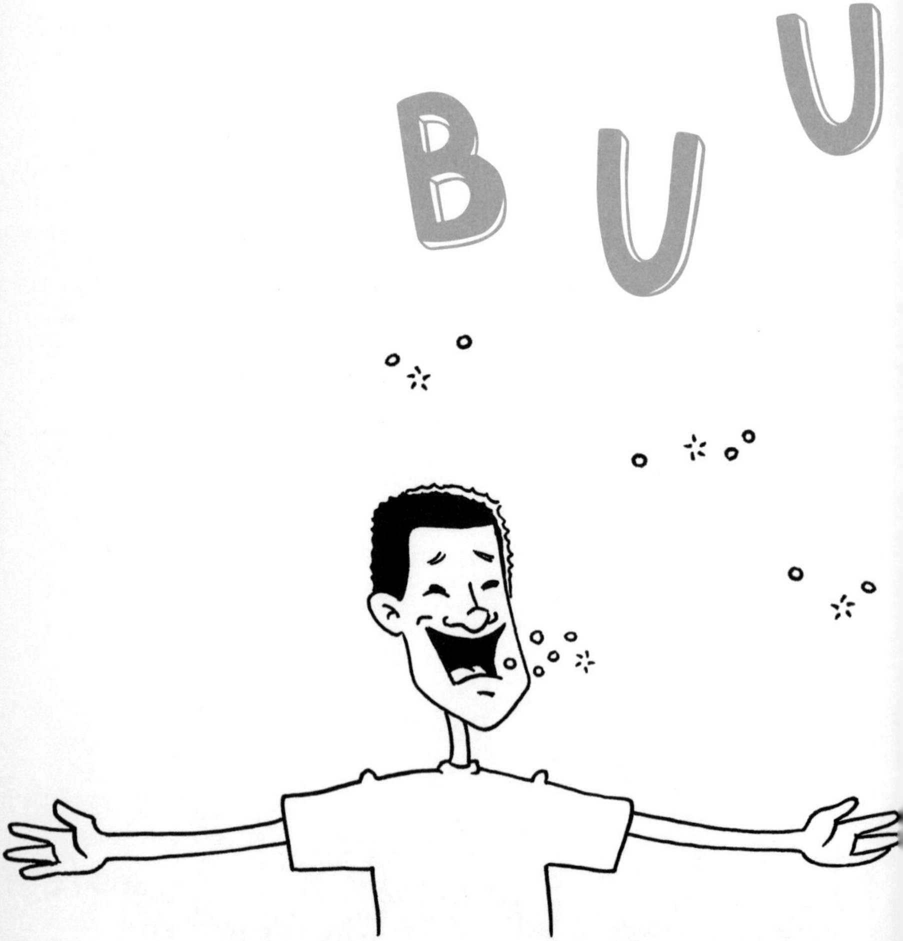
BUU

UURRR

still going!

RRRRP

finally finished!

Dad can also **fart** from the **front door** to the **back door** but we won't go into that.

The other thing Dad likes to do is **dance really badly**. He tries to copy people on TV.

horsey dance

worm dance

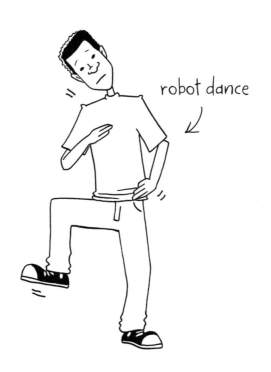

robot dance

still the worm dance

Finally, there's Granddad. His teeth come out and his body parts make **funny** noises...

WHOOP WHOOP!

And he likes to play **silly** tricks.

《SHAKE》 HANDS?

ZZZZZ
ZZZZZ
ZZZZZZ!

HAHA
HAHAHA

He also pulls his pants up **really high** which is the opposite to some of the **cool** kids at school.

Granddad—
high

Joey Keenan—
low

Toby
Hogan—
super
low

Even our **pet bird** is weird. Most birds like to make happy chirpy noises. But **Blockhead** always makes strange sounds, like ...

WOOF WOOF!

And sometimes...

MOOO!

And if he's eaten some funny bird seed he'll say...

WANNA FIGHT?

Henry's my best friend from school. He doesn't care that I'm weird, or that I like to draw silly pictures.

Like this one...

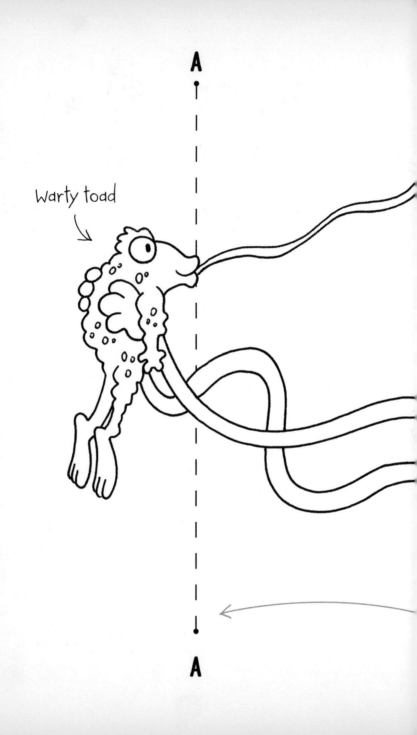

A

Warty toad

A

Me and Henry like to make up new words for things, too ... like **'Finkles'**.

That's the word we invented for the **wrinkles** you get on your **fingers** when you've sat in the bath

for

<u>too</u>

long.

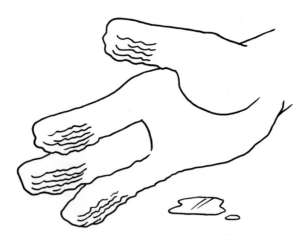

We reckon if we say it enough everyone will start to use it,

even the Queen.

CHAPTER 3

Bella's party is two days away, so I want to be as **normal** as possible at school to make sure that she won't **un-invite** me.

This was going to be hard since today we were going on a school excursion to the **ZOO** and Granddad was coming as a teacher's helper.

I knew it was going to be **trouble** when Granddad showed up at breakfast wearing fake **monkey ears**.

When we got on the **school bus**, Granddad
took the empty seat next to Henry, and the
only seat left for me was next to ...

Bella.

I like Bella. I like her **a lot**. But I'm not sure if
I'm ready to sit next to her on a bus.

We said hi . . .

HI BELLA

... and that's it!

I didn't know what else to say to her. She didn't know what else to say to me. We just sat there **staring** at the back of the heads of the people in front of us!

Henry

Granddad/ monkey

The sight of Granddad's **monkey ears** and Henry's **fuzzy orange hair** gave me an idea.

I took out my sketchbook and started **drawing** ...

'What are you drawing?' Bella asked.

IT'S A MONKEYLION!

Bella reached down into her bag and pulled out a pair of **glasses**. She put them on and looked closely at my drawing.

HA! IT'S FUNNY. YOU'RE A GOOD DRAWER, WEIR.

I hadn't seen Bella wearing glasses before, and I must have been staring at them because she noticed.

'The glasses are new,' said Bella. 'The eye doctor said I need to wear them when I'm looking at something closely.'

'**Cool**,' I said. 'Can I try them on?'

SURE

She took them off and put them on **me**.

The glasses made **everything** look different.

They made Granddad's ears look

even bigger.

And Henry's head was **HUGE!**

You **do not** want to know what Toby Hogan looked like ...

That was when Bella
asked me to draw her.

WEIR,
CAN YOU
DRAW ME?

YES!

This was my chance to **impress** Bella with the one thing that I'm

really good at!

I picked up my sketchbook and pencil and started drawing Bella as well as I could.

When I finished, I showed her the picture of herself.

THAT'S . . .
UMM NICE,
WEIR . . .

Bella said it was nice but I don't think she meant it, because she had the same look on her face that Mum had when she found that dead mouse in the laundry basket . . .

THAT'S . . .
UMM . . .
NOT NICE.

Then I realised...

Oh no!

I **forgot** to take off the glasses and they made me draw her **really <u>badly</u>**!

Oh man... What a way to start the day.

CHAPTER 4

When we got to the **zoo**, the first animals we saw were the **monkeys**.

I love monkeys, so me and Granddad went right up close to the fence.

I thought Granddad's monkey ears looked
silly but the monkeys must have thought
they looked real, because the first thing that
happened was

a monkey

threw a banana

right at Granddad!

Granddad ducked out of the way.

Then I ducked out of the way.

And the **banana** hit Henry…

right in the

It was **sooo** funny, I started laughing.

HAHA!!!!!!!!

I was **laughing**

so hard

I didn't see the **second banana** that was thrown.

Bella ducked it.

Blake ducked it.

Toby Hogan ducked it.

And it hit **me**
right on the side
of the head!

Now **everyone** was laughing at **me**!
Even Granddad!

HA HA HA HA HA HA

64

I guess it looked **pretty funny**!

As Henry and me stood there **flicking** the banana off ourselves, a whole bunch of **ducks** ran up to eat the bits off the ground.

They were funny, those ducks. Fat ones, skinny ones, and a big spotty one.

The **spotty** one had three little ducklings following it,

which was **very cute**.

Bella gave me a **hanky** to wipe myself. 'Here you go, Weir,' she said.

'Thanks,' I said. And that's when I realised the hanky had **little frogs** on it.

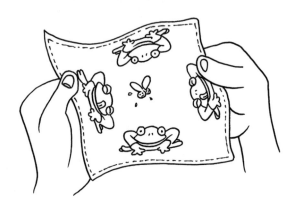

I looked up and Bella was **smiling**.

Soon it was lunchtime, which was perfect cos I had heaps of ideas for cool animal pictures. First I tried a

giraffe and a kangaroo.

A Giraffaroo!

A **zebra** and an **elephant** …

A Zelephant!

A **panda** and a **gorilla** ...

A Pandarilla!

But then I decided I wanted to try another drawing of Bella. I quickly drew her while she watched Henry

pretending he was a

sea lion.

I was pretty happy with my drawing and knew Bella would like it much more than the last one.

But as I went to hand it to her,

the skinny duck waddled over and

 snatched it

away from me! >>>>

Before I knew it, Bella had jumped up and was chasing after the duck with my drawing in its bill!

I ran after her.

I might have mentioned that I'm **not** a very fast runner...

And it turns out that duck was a
very fast waddler! 》》》

We chased that duck down past
the **gorilla** enclosure, 》》》

through the **bat** cave, ▷▷▷

along the **penguin** pool... ▷▷▷

But then we lost the duck around

the **meerkat** bend.

Not only had we lost the duck,

but now we were lost too!

We couldn't find Granddad, Miss Franklin, or anyone from school...

so we found the next BEST thing...

'Hey,' said Bella, 'what are you going to wear to **my party**?'

Huh? I thought to myself.

YOU KNOW IT'S A DRESS-UP PARTY, DON'T YOU?

'Oh yeah,' I replied. 'Sure ... I'm going to go as ...'

'So what was your drawing of, anyway?' asked Bella.

'Oh, nothing,' I replied. 'Just an—'

'BELLA ALLEN!' the zoo loudspeaker suddenly boomed.

BELLA ALLEN,
PLEASE RETURN TO
THE ZOO KIOSK
TO MEET YOUR TEACHER,
MISS FRANKLIN.

'AND WEIRDO!' the loudspeaker continued.

HAS ANYONE SEEN A WEIRDO? HE WAS LAST SEEN WEARING A BLUE SHIRT, GREY SHORTS, AND HIS BIG SISTER'S SHOES. COULD WEIRDO PLEASE RETURN TO THE MONKEY ENCLOSURE?

Everyone at the zoo laughed.

All the animals too.

The monkeys ...

The **penguins** . . .

Even the **duck** with the **glasses**!

I wanted to run away and hide, but before I could make a move, Granddad appeared.

I KNEW I'D FIND YOU NEAR THE FROGS!

The day at the zoo

wasn't a complete disaster.

On my way out, I found the perfect birthday present for Bella in the gift shop...

TWO ROBOTS

At school the next day, Miss Franklin told us that we all needed to draw a picture of someone else in the class.

Here was my chance to draw Bella again!

But then Bella asked Henry if he would be her partner!

HENRY.

HENRY.

HENRY!!!

So I wound up with Clare instead . . .

I thought I'd done a

pretty good job

of my drawing.

Henry's drawing of Bella was even worse than mine from the bus!

Bella

by Henry

After school, Henry invited me over to his place to work on our costumes for Bella's party.

Henry was going as a **computer**. He put a box on his head and I helped him attach a keyboard to his chest. When we finished he looked like a human iPad.

He had lots of green cardboard for me to use to make a frog hat.

Perfect!

When we were finished, Henry showed me his **COLLECTION OF ROCKS** that he'd made to look like things...

...and then he introduced me to his sister.

'**WEIRDO?**' said Jane. 'That's not very nice.'

'Oh no, that's his name,' said Henry.

'Yeah, it's actually my name,' I said.

Then I met Henry's twin brothers. They looked <u>exactly</u> the same!

'I can see that,' I said.

They even **talked** the same.

PEOPLE SAY THEY CAN'T TELL US APART.

PEOPLE SAY THEY CAN'T TELL US APART.

I couldn't tell them apart!

WE ARE DIFFERENT IN SOME WAYS, THOUGH.

WE ARE DIFFERENT IN SOME WAYS, THOUGH.

HE LIKES TO EAT GREEN M&M'S
AND I LIKE TO EAT BLUE M&M'S.

YEAH, HE LIKES TO EAT BLUE M&M'S AND I LIKE TO EAT GREEN M&M'S.

It was like looking at **two robots**.

Then Henry's mum and dad and their dog came out.

So this is what a _normal family_ looks like!

'It's dinner time, boys,' said Mr O'Henry.
'Come join us at the table.'

My mum and dad's dinners <u>**never**</u>
look how they're supposed to.

How
spaghetti is
supposed
to look

How Mum's
spaghetti
looks

How a baked dinner is supposed to look

How Dad's baked dinner looks

How noodles are supposed to look

How Granddad's 'noodles' look

...but they always taste delicious!

But Mrs O'Henry's roast looked **just like** the picture in the book!

YUUUUUM!

This is going to be SUPER yummy, I thought to myself.

Shame it **tasted** like **cardboard**!

BIG CUCUMBER!

CHAPTER 6

Today is Bella's **birthday party**!

Bella's present is wrapped...

and my **green** clothes are ready...

My **frog** hat is—

'HEY,' I said, 'where's my frog hat?'

Then I heard a

TERRIBLE

SPLASH!

coming from
the **bathroom**.

where
my frog
hat
SHOULD
have
been!

ROGER!

NOOOOO

I ran to the bathroom but it was **too late**.
My frog hat was already

sinking

in

bathwater…

I fished it out, and it

fell apart

in my hands.

I looked at Roger…

=CLEAN!=

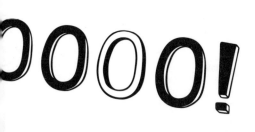

OOOO!

WEIR,
YOU CAN STILL
WEAR YOUR
GREEN
PYJAMAS.

'I can't just wear green,'
I complained. 'I'll look like
a **BIG** cucumber!'

Great, I get invited to
Bella's party and now
I can't even go...

Then Sally stepped into
the bathroom with an
'excellent idea'.

I HAVE AN
EXCELLENT IDEA!

She pointed to the piles and piles of **toilet rolls** in the corner.

Sally is supposed to be the **clever** one, but this was the

worst idea ever!

'Sally, I'm **not** going as a **toilet roll**!' I said.

Sally groaned. 'No, we can wrap you with it, like a **mummy**!'

She picked up a roll and started **spinning** me around and around and around . . . and when I finally stopped whirling, I looked in the mirror and saw . . .

a really

COOL

mummy!

'Not bad,' I said. 'Thanks!'

So we're finally on our way to Bella's place, when we start

running out of petrol.

But instead of stopping at the first petrol station we see, Dad wants to wait until we come across a **cheaper** one!

Sometimes Dad can be **just as cheap** as Mum!

Can you guess what happened next?

We ran out of petrol!

So Dad orders us all out, to help push >>>> the car, while Granddad runs off to get us a can of petrol.

First my frog hat gets destroyed, then our car runs out of petrol on our way to the party...

What could be worse?

RAIN!

Rain could be worse!

Granddad came back with petrol, just as the rain stopped. But I no longer looked like a mummy...

I looked like a kid who'd been

FLUSHED down the toilet!

And my hands were covered in

FINKLES!

'What now?' I asked my genius sister.

DON'T ASK ME!

I climbed back into the car. I looked in the boot behind me and saw the mega bag of chips and the huge packet of safety pins that Roger had snuck into Mum's trolley.

Roger's shopping had just given me

a BRILLIANT idea!

SNABBIT!

CHAPTER 7

I turned myself into a **vending machine**!

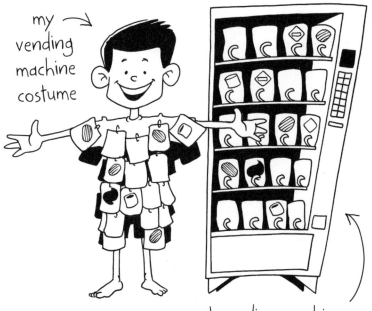

my →
vending
machine
costume

real vending machine

Everyone loved it, especially Bella's mum.
She'd forgotten to pick up all the **party snacks**,
so I'd arrived at just the right time...

MINE!
CHIPS!
OOH!
YUM!
MMM!
CHIPS!
YUM!
SALT AND VINEGAR!
MY FAVOURITE!

The only downside was that Toby Hogan tried to **pay for the chips** by putting a **coin** in my **ear**...

There was supposed to be a **magician** at the party, but he couldn't come because his **rabbit** had **eaten** his car keys.

MY CAR KEYS
HAVE
DISAPPEARED.

HIC!

HIC!

But that didn't matter too much, because there was something at the party that turned out to be much more fun than a magician.

My crazy, weird family.

Granddad was up first to do some tricks. He pulled out his teeth ...

I CAN MAKE MY TEETH DISAPPEAR!

Then he made them _____! ←vanish

WOW!

Next, he said

WATCH MY
MAGIC
ELBOW

Then **Dad** was up.

I NEED A FIZZY DRINK.

UH-OH.

I started to **panic**. What was he going to do?

Dad burped his way through

HAPPY BIRTHDAYYY

Then some **music** came on the radio and **Dad started doing his**

<u>horsey</u> dance.

Roger

Toby Hogan   Mary   Mullet   Sally

Soon **EVERYONE** was joining in.

Bella

Me

Granddad

Mum

Dad

Next, **Sally** started making some **cool balloon animals** for everyone.

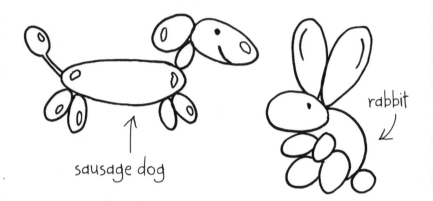

sausage dog

rabbit

Then I made the only **balloon animal** that I knew how to.

IT'S A SNAKE!

snake

Then I came up with

another GREAT idea!

I tied **my snake** to **Sally's rabbit** and made a **super cool** animal.

snabbit

A SNABBIT!

It was turning out to be a **great party**! I did a **BIG drawing** and we had a game of

pin the tail on the donkey-pottamus

Roger helped Bella blow out her birthday candles, and Granddad laughed so loudly that his teeth

flew out

and landed in . . .

the lolly bowl.

Henry thought they were lolly teeth and was just about to grab them when I scooped them up. 'HENRY!
HENRY!!
HENRY!!!' I said.

'Huh?'

'Believe me, they're **NOT** as tasty as they look!'

Boy, that was close!

But before long, everyone was taking their balloon animals and saying goodbye.

Then I spotted Roger dropping leftover cake into the fruit juice.

CLEAN!

I was trying to **scoop** the cake out when Bella came up to us.

'He is **sooooo** cute,' said Bella.

Cute? Roger?

I handed him to Mum.

'I'm really glad you came to my party, Weir,' Bella added. 'You know, your drawing of Clare yesterday was really nice.'

'Thanks,' I said.

'You drew me, on the bus, but I guess I'm not as nice-looking as her ...'

HUH?
OH NO, YOU ARE!
I JUST . . .
IT WAS . . .

THE PROBLEM WAS YOUR GLASSES . . .

'Oh!' said Bella.

'Hey, I almost forgot to give you this,' I said, remembering the present in my pocket that I'd found for her at the zoo.

First, Bella opened the card I'd made her.

Bella blushed and gave me a **great big smile**.

I'm a bit short and I can't run very fast, but I'm **lucky** I can draw.

She opened the present next.

WOW, I LOVE IT!

'Thanks, Weir,' she said. 'You're the best. And thanks for saving my party. It looked like it was going to be a disaster...

...UNTIL YOU AND YOUR FAMILY SHOWED UP.

Phew. I'd made it through my **first birthday party** with my <u>new</u> friends.

And the **seventh-best-looking girl** in school just called me

THE BEST.

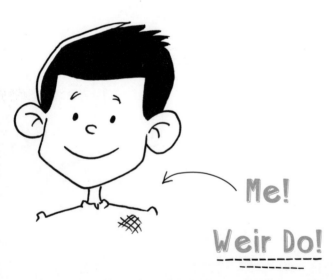

Me!

Weir Do!

For my three **boys**

who helped me with

this book...

FROM ANH

★ Henry's **funny-looking** mum and dad, based on drawings by **Xavier Do**

★ Henry's **strange** twin brothers, based on drawings by **Luc Do**

★ **Blockhead** the parrot's crazy habits, suggested by **Leon Do**

ACKNOWLEDGEMENTS

FROM JULES

For Connor Maclean, the **strongest** kid I've ever known

Weir Do's the new kid in school. With an **unforgettable** name, a **crazy** family and some seriously **weird** habits, fitting in won't be easy... but it will be **FUNNY!**

bird

Book 1

GOT IT!

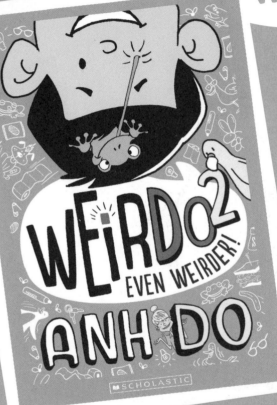

COLLECT THEM ALL!

YOU CAN NEVER HAVE TOO MANY WEIRDOS

Book 2

GOT IT!

monkey

flying banana

SEE YA
SOON!